HOW MANY SLEEPS
till my Birthday?

written by

Mark Sperr...

illustrated by

...astien Braun

One summer's morning, when the birds were busy
waking the world with a song, Little Pip climbed out of bed,
padded across the floor and . . .

"PSSST!" He gave Daddy Grizzle
a BIG bear shake. "Daddy Grizzle,
WAKE UP!" said Little Pip.
"Today is a very special day."

"That's nice," mumbled
Daddy Grizzle.

"Yes," said Little Pip, "because today is my birthday . . ."
(For a moment the birds fell silent.)

"Your birthday??!!!!" gasped Daddy Grizzle, his eyes flashing open.

Then **THUD,** he jumped out of bed and dashed out the door.

"But WAIT," said Daddy Grizzle. "Today isn't your birthday. There are still **THREE** whole sleeps till your birthday."

"Really . . . ?" sighed Little Pip.

"Really," nodded Daddy Grizzle, "but, seeing that we're up, let's go out anyway."

So out they went into the woods and carefully collected some branches and twigs.

That night, tucked up tight,
Little Pip thought he heard
the *rasp* of a saw and the
tap of a hammer before . . .

ZZZZZZZZZ

he fell fast asleep.

The next morning, when Daddy Grizzle was still snoozing, Little Pip gave him a shake.

"PSSST! Wake up, Daddy Grizzle!" he said.
"I think it's my birthday!"

Daddy Grizzle's eyes POPPED open.

HOW TO MAKE...

Then he threw off
his blanket,

grabbed a basket . . .

and *rushed* out
the door.

*B*ut no sooner had he gone outside than Daddy Grizzle
remembered something *rather* important and,
with a BIG bear GROAN, he turned himself
around and headed back.

"**N**o, Little Pip," sighed Daddy Grizzle, "today is NOT your birthday. In fact, there are **TWO** whole sleeps until your birthday."

"Really . . . ?" sighed Little Pip.

"**Really**," sighed Daddy Grizzle, "but, now that we're up, let's go out anyway."

So out they went and filled their baskets with all the loveliest things the woods had to offer.

When they got home later that day,
Daddy Grizzle reminded Little Pip just
how many sleeps there were until his birthday.

And that night, as Little Pip stirred
from the sweetest of dreams,
he thought he *sniffed* a whiff of
something wonderful before . . .

Z Z Z Z Z z z z z z z

falling back to sleep.

The next day, Little Pip (what a clever bear) *somehow* remembered it was NOT his birthday that day.

Little Pip,
GO back to sleep.
It's **NOT** your birthday,
thanks
Daddy Grizzle xxx

But "PSSST!" he still had a
very important question to ask . . .

"Daddy Grizzle! Daddy Grizzle!
HOW MANY SLEEPS
till my birthday?"

Daddy Grizzle rose
sleepily from his pillow.
"Little Pip," he yawned,
"only ONE sleep to go."

And, seeing as they were both now awake,
up they got and out they went . . .

And, while Little Pip kept himself busy with all sorts of things, Daddy Grizzle handed out some very important invitations.

That night, before bed, Little Pip thought he might burst with excitement. "HOW MANY SLEEPS till my **birthday**?" he asked.

"*One*," whispered Daddy Grizzle.
"Just *one*."

And, as Little Pip drifted
off to sleep,

ZZZZZZZZZ

he thought he heard
a little POP.

The following morning,
Little Pip knew EXACTLY
what day it was.

But, when he went to wake up Daddy Grizzle,
all he found was a little note . . .

So, Little Pip followed the balloons out of the house, down the path . . .

He followed them into the woods, through the stream, SPLiSh! SPLaSh! SPLoSh!

. . . and over the bridge.

And right the way past the – WhOoPs! PoP! – berry bushes, until . . .

Well, Little Pip couldn't have wished for a better surprise or a lovelier birthday. All his friends were there and everything was wonderful!

And later . . . much later, when the cake
had been eaten and the games had been played,
Little Pip charged about with a chuckle and a cheer.
Then Daddy Grizzle smiled and said . . .

"Who knows . . .
tomorrow morning we might even have
a lovely long LIE-IN. *How nice.*"

But the next morning, before the birds had even sung
a single note, a little voice said loudly,

"Pssst! Daddy Grizzle!
Daddy Grizzle!

Wake up!
WAKE UP . . .
HOW MANY SLEEPS
till Christmas?”

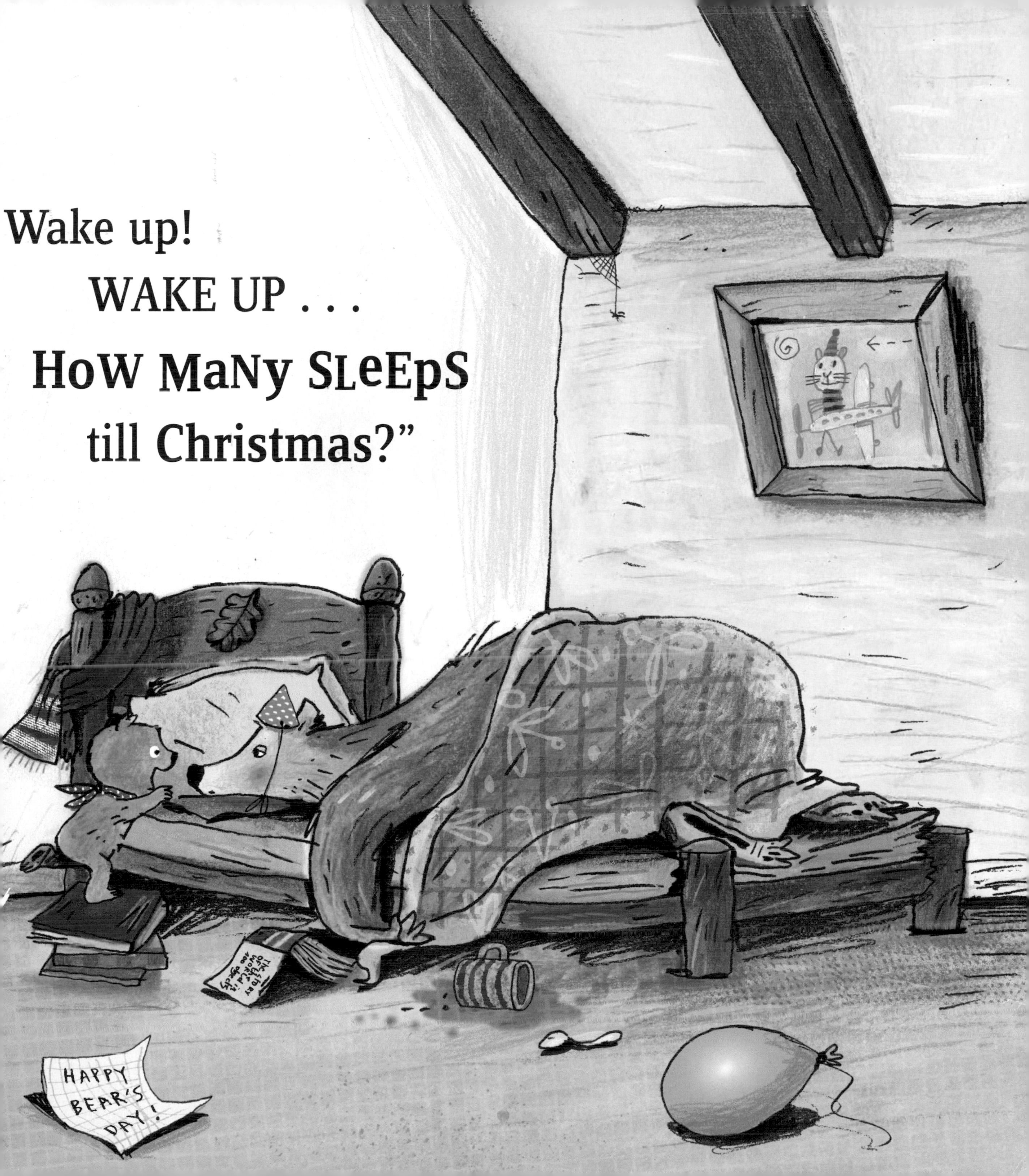

For Louise with much and many thanks - M. S.

To Cath, the best party organizer ever - S. B.

PUFFIN BOOKS
Published by the Penguin Group: London, New York,
Australia, Canada, India, Ireland, New Zealand and South Africa
Penguin Books Ltd, Registered Offices: 80 Strand, London WC2R 0RL, England
puffinbooks.com
First published 2013
001
Text copyright © Mark Sperring, 2013
Illustrations copyright © Sébastien Braun, 2013
All rights reserved
The moral right of the author and illustrator has been asserted
Made and printed in China
ISBN: 978–0–718–19657–8